if i had a DRAGON

Written and illustrated by Tom and Amanda Ellery

SIMON & SCHUSTER BOOKS FOR YOUNG READERS

New York   London   Toronto   Sydney

To our parents, who inspired us when we were young, and to our three Mortons—Tommy, Johnny, and Katie—who inspire us today.

And to Alisha Niehaus and Daniel Roode—for making it happen.

 SIMON & SCHUSTER BOOKS FOR YOUNG READERS

An imprint of Simon & Schuster Children's Publishing Division

1230 Avenue of the Americas, New York, New York 10020

Copyright © 2006 by Tom and Amanda Ellery

SIMON & SCHUSTER BOOKS FOR YOUNG READERS is a trademark of Simon & Schuster, Inc.

Book design by Daniel Roode

The text for this book is set in Albatross.

The illustrations for this book are rendered in charcoal, ink, and watercolor.

Manufactured in Mexico

10 9 8 7 6 5 4 3 2 1

Library of Congress Cataloging-in-Publication Data

Ellery, Amanda.

If I had a dragon / written and illustrated by Amanda & Tom Ellery.—1st ed.

p. cm.

Summary: Tired of playing with his little brother, a boy imagines having a dragon for a playmate instead.

ISBN-13: 978-1-4169-0924-8

ISBN-10: 1-4169-0924-9

[1. Brothers—Fiction. 2. Dragons—Fiction. 3. Play—Fiction.]

I. Ellery, Tom. II. Title.

PZ7.E42848If 2006

[E]—dc22   2005017978

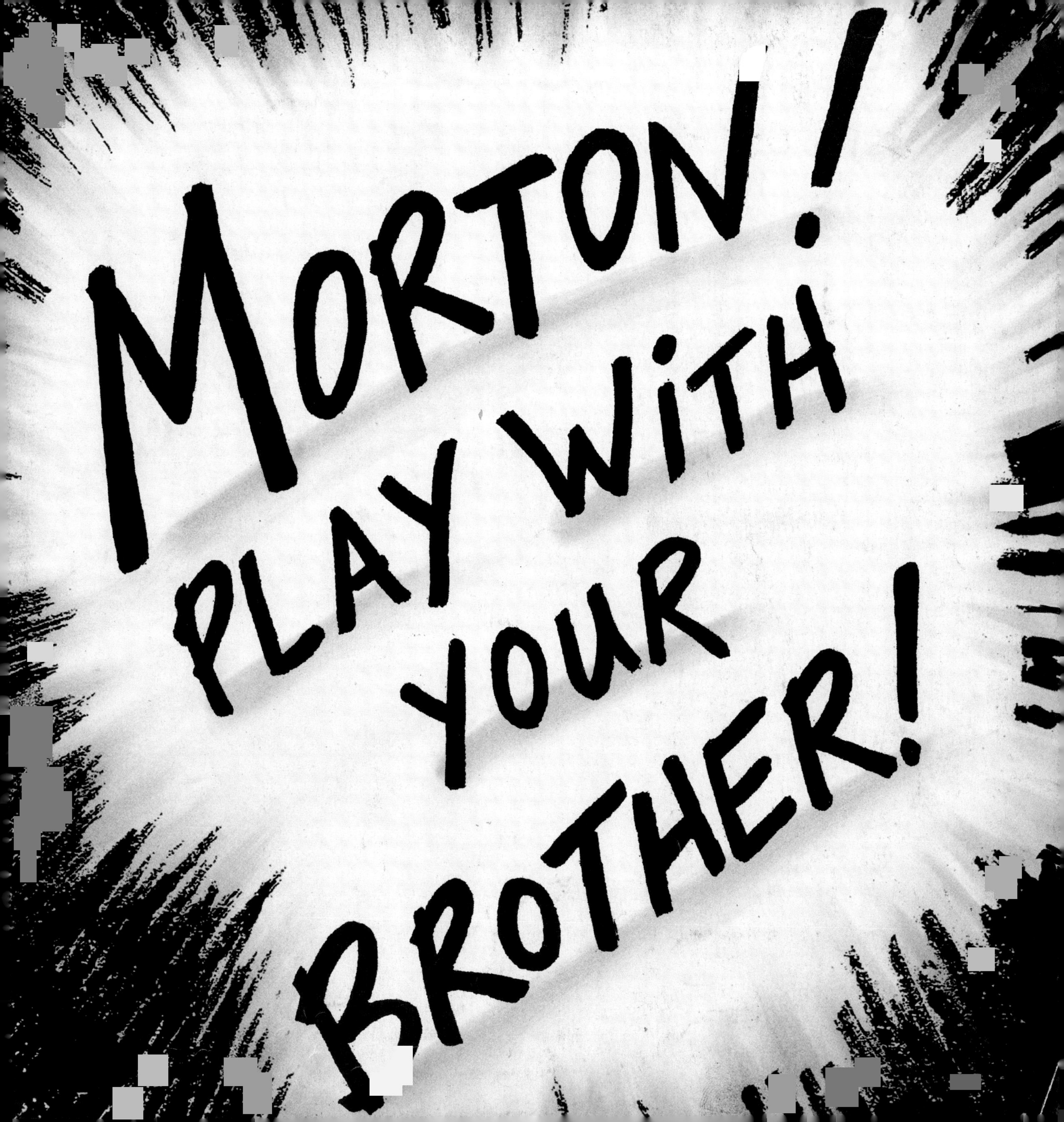
MORTON! PLAY WITH YOUR BROTHER!

I don't want to play with my brother! He's too little.

I wish he would turn into
something fun . . .

. . . like a new kite,

...a DRAGON!

If I had a dragon, I would be so happy. We could go for walks. . . .

We could play basketball!

Go for a swim?

Ready or not, here I . . .

. . . come.

A movie?

I guess a dragon doesn't
make a very good playmate
after all.